The Tiara Club

at Diamond Turrets

For Sydney Rose Fordham
and her special friends xxx
VF
With very special thanks to JD

www.tiaraclub.co.uk

ORCHARD BOOKS
338 Euston Road, London NW1 3BH
Orchard Books Australia
Level 17/207 Kent St, Sydney, NSW 2000

A Paperback Original
First published in Great Britain in 2009
Text © Vivian French 2009
Cover illustration © Sarah Gibb 2009
Inside illustrations © Orchard Books 2009

The right of Vivian French to be identified as the author of this
work has been asserted by her in accordance with the Copyright,
Designs and Patents Act 1988.

A CIP catalogue record for this book is available
from the British Library.

ISBN 978 1 84616 880 2

1 3 5 7 9 10 8 6 4 2

Printed in Great Britain

Orchard Books is a division of Hachette Children's Books,
an Hachette UK company.

www.hachette.co.uk

The Tiara Club

at Diamond Turrets

Princess Rebecca

and the Lion Cub

By Vivian French

ORCHARD BOOKS

The Royal Palace Academy
for the Preparation of Perfect Princesses

(Known to our students as "*The Princess Academy*")

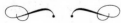

OUR SCHOOL MOTTO:
*A Perfect Princess always thinks of others
before herself, and is kind, caring and truthful.*

Diamond Turrets offers a complete education for
Tiara Club princesses, focusing on caring for animals
and the environment. The curriculum includes:

*A visit to the Royal
County Show*

*Visits to the Country
Park and Bamboo Grove*

*Work experience on our
very own farm*

*Elephant rides in our
Safari Park (students
will be closely supervised)*

Our headteacher, King Percy, is present at all times, and
students are well looked after by Fairy G, the school
Fairy Godmother.

Our resident staff and visiting experts include:

*LADY WHITSTABLE-KENT
(IN CHARGE OF THE FARM,
COUNTRY PARK AND SAFARI PARK)*

*FAIRY ANGORA
(ASSISTANT FAIRY GODMOTHER)*

*FARMER KATE
(DOMESTIC ANIMALS)*

*QUEEN MOTHER MATILDA
(ETIQUETTE, POSTURE AND
APPEARANCE)*

*LADY MAY (SUPERVISOR OF THE
HOLIDAY HOME FOR PETS)*

We award tiara points to encourage our Tiara Club princesses towards the next level. All princesses who win enough points at Diamond Turrets will be presented with their Diamond Sashes and attend a celebration ball.

Diamond Sash Tiara Club princesses are invited to return to Golden Gates, our magnificent mansion residence for Perfect Princesses, where they may continue their education at a higher level.

PLEASE NOTE:
Princesses are expected to arrive at the Academy with a *minimum* of:

Twenty ballgowns
(with all necessary hoops, petticoats, etc)

Twelve day dresses

Seven gowns
suitable for garden parties and other special day occasions

Twelve tiaras

Dancing shoes
five pairs

Velvet slippers
three pairs

Riding boots
two pairs

Wellington boots, waterproof cloaks and other essential protective clothing as required

Oh no...I'm sure I'm going to do
this wrong! Please excuse me if I do –
sometimes I get in a terrible fluster
about things if I haven't done them
before. Are you like that? It's so nice
to know you're here with us at Diamond
Turrets. Have you met the other Tulip
Room princesses yet? There's Abigail
and Caitlin, Bethany and Lindsey...but
that's only four. Oops! I've forgotten
Mia! And now you've met me, too.
I'm Princess Rebecca...

Chapter One

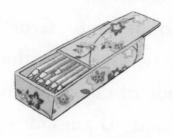

We were AMAZED when Caitlin said it was only a week until the end of term. And shocked as well...

"Oh no!" Mia gasped. "Does that mean King Percy's counting up our tiara points already? What if we haven't got enough?"

"Don't worry, Mia," I said. "It will be OK," and I patted her hand.

I'm sure we'll all get our lovely
Diamond Sashes at the end of
term celebration."

Diamonde and Gruella, the
horrible twins, were sitting on the
other side of the recreation room
table, and Diamonde snorted

loudly. "I wouldn't be too sure about that," she said, and there was a nasty gleam in her eye. "I heard Lady Whitstable-Kent talking to King Percy, and they were saying how disappointed they were with the results this year. And I think Lady Whit mentioned your name, Rebecca!"

King Percy is our headteacher, but Lady Whitstable-Kent looks after the animals and our outdoor lessons here at Diamond Turrets. She can be quite scary, and she doesn't hesitate to say if we aren't working hard enough. My stomach turned over and I felt sick, but Bethany leant across the table. "What do you mean, you think she mentioned Rebecca?" she asked. "Did she mention her or didn't she?"

Diamonde frowned. "I couldn't hear properly. But it did sound as

if she was talking about Rebecca, didn't it, Gruella?"

Gruella nodded, and I felt my stomach flip over again. Lindsey looked thoughtfully at the twins. "So where exactly were you when you heard this?"

Diamonde started rattling the pencils in her pencil box, and Gruella went pink. "Oh – just in the corridor," she said, but she sounded suspiciously guilty. "Weren't we, Diamonde? We were just walking along, and we heard Lady Whit, so we stopped and—"

"No we didn't!" Diamonde interrupted her sister. "We went on walking past. Has anyone got a pencil sharpener? No? Well, I'm going to go and find one. Come on, Gruella. You can help me." And she jumped up from the table and dragged Gruella away with her.

Abigail rolled her eyes. "They've been listening outside a door again," she said. "I can tell."

"I bet they didn't really hear anything." Caitlin gave me an encouraging smile. "You know what they're like – they just enjoy being nasty."

I tried to smile back, but I was worried. What if everyone else was awarded a sash, and I wasn't? It would be TOO awful if I didn't get to go to Golden Gates with my friends. We've been together for ages and ages – I don't know what I'd do without them! I was about

to try and work out how many tiara points I had when the door burst wide open and Katie came rushing in.

"Have you HEARD?" she gasped. "We're going to see the lions in the Safari Park tomorrow, and we're going to ride on ELEPHANTS!

The elephants can go really, really close to the lions so we can see them properly – it's SO exciting!" Katie stopped to take a quick breath, then went on, "I can hardly believe it! I've been waiting to see the lions all term, but we never got to go – but now we can! AND there are lion cubs! Lady Whit told me to tell you. She says we're all to have an early breakfast, and then we'll be off. Oh, isn't it just TOO wonderful?"

Chapter Two

It took me ages and ages to get to sleep that night, and when I finally did I had the weirdest dream. I dreamt I was the only princess not to get her Diamond Sash and Fairy G sent me home in disgrace. And she didn't send me home in a coach; I had to ride on an elephant, and it kept going the wrong way. When I told the others in the morning Bethany laughed so much she nearly fell out of bed.

"Honestly, Rebecca! You really do have the funniest dreams ever!" she chortled.

Mia was more sympathetic. "Poor old you," she said. "You should have told us you couldn't get to sleep. When my little sister won't shut her eyes I sing to her, and she's asleep in seconds."

Caitlin grinned at me. "Do stop worrying about your tiara points. If YOU haven't got enough then NONE of us has, so we'll all be together whatever happens." That made me feel loads better, and I felt quite cheerful as we hurried along the corridor for breakfast.

As soon as we'd finished, Lady Whit came into the dining hall with Fairy G and her assistant,

Fairy Angora. Lady Whit was carrying a big clipboard, and looked stern.

"There will be eight of you on each elephant," she announced, "together with a teacher. You will be quite safe if you do exactly as you are told. I expect you all to be sensible, and at the end of the day you will write a report, including a detailed description of the lions." Lady Whit put her clipboard down as if she had finished, but Fairy G whispered in her ear, and Lady Whit nodded. "There will, of course, be tiara points awarded for the best entries. This is a golden opportunity for you to increase your total score, and I think it only fair to tell you that some of you are in SERIOUS need of extra points."

At once my stomach started doing somersaults, and I could see Lindsey biting her lip.

"Wow!" Abigail whispered as Lady Whit strode out. "That's so SCARY!"

Mia folded her arms. "We'll be OK," she said firmly. "Let's just make sure we do the best reports we possibly can!"

Bethany jumped to her feet. "Why don't we all make notes, and then we can share the information at the end of the day?"

"All for one and one for all," Caitlin agreed, and we smiled at each other as we made our way to the recreation room to collect our notebooks.

The twins were already there, and Diamonde sneered as we came in. "Oooh! It's the Tulips!

I hope you're going to help poor little Rebecca get a few more tiara points! Lady Whit was looking at her all the time she was talking, wasn't she, Gruella?"

Gruella looked blank. "Was she?"

"Of course she was!" Diamonde scowled at her sister. "Now do hurry up." And she stomped off out through the door.

It was such a beautiful day we didn't need cloaks or wraps. We lined up outside the school front door in our groups, and we were SO thrilled when Fairy Angora said she was coming with us.

We weren't nearly so pleased when we realised the twins were coming too, but we tried not to show how we felt. Caitlin murmured, "A Perfect Princess is kind and gracious to everyone – even the twins," and I tried not to giggle as they walked towards us. At once Diamonde started boasting that she knew ALL about lions, but she stopped as the elephants came into sight...and we all stood and stared and STARED.

Chapter Three

Have you ever ridden on an elephant? I hadn't. I'd never even been close to one before, and I hadn't realised just how huge they are, and how dignified. They came swaying towards us, one behind the other, and they looked AMAZING. There were beautiful red feathery plumes on their heads, and wonderfully decorated seats on their backs that looked like satin benches heaped with cushions.

"However will we get up there?"
Lindsey asked anxiously, but Fairy
Angora squeezed her arm.

"Don't worry, petal," she said,
and a moment later she waved her
wand...and there was an arch, with
steps up either side. Each elephant
stopped under the arch in turn and
we scrambled up and onto the
seats – it felt SO high up! I looked
down to see how Lindsey was
going to manage, and saw Fairy G
twirling her magic wand again;
a second later Lindsey was safely
tucked in between me and Bethany.

"I'm ever so glad there's a rail,"
Bethany whispered, and I had to
admit I was glad too, although
I was certain Fairy Angora would
never let anything happen to us.

"Everyone ready?" Fairy G called, and off we went. The twins screamed as we began to move, but it really wasn't frightening once you got used to it. We held on tightly to the rail to begin with, but quite soon we were sitting

upright and chatting as usual. It didn't feel as if we were going fast, but in no time we were through the country park and passing the Bamboo Grove...and then we were going through the massive iron gates of the Safari Park.

"Here we are," Fairy Angora announced, and we held our breath as the gates swung open. Our elephant was the last to go through, and when the gates clanged shut behind us I saw him twitch his ears.

"I wonder who'll see a lion first," Caitlin said as we swung over the top of a mound and began to make our way in between tall clumps of spiky grass.

"I will, of course," Diamonde boasted. "Mummy says I've got wonderful eyesight." She turned round to look behind her, and then let out a sudden squeal, "QUICK! Over there!"

We all looked to see what she was pointing at, and I don't think any of us expected to see a lion...but for once Diamonde was right.

There was a sunny patch of grass surrounded by boulders, and a lioness was lying half in and half out of the shadows. Beside her two roly-poly cubs were tumbling about...they looked GORGEOUS!

"Oh!" We hardly dared to breathe. Fairy Angora whispered in the elephant's ear and he stood as still as a rock while we watched the lion cubs play. The lioness looked up a couple of times, but she didn't seem to be bothered by us being there. One of the cubs was much braver than the other, and it was difficult not to laugh out loud as he clambered up to the top of the biggest boulder and then jumped off in a totally "Look at me! I'm so clever!" kind of way.

Mia quietly found her pencil and

notebook and began to make some notes, and Abigail did the same. Gruella gave a shrill shriek of laughter.

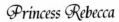

"Oooh! What goody-goodies!
Do look, Diamonde!"

At once the lioness stood up with a low growl and the brave little lion cub, who had just reached the top of his boulder, lost his balance and fell. I thought he'd jump up again, but he didn't. He tried to, but every time he put his paw to the ground he whimpered.

His mother licked his head and gave him a gentle nudge, but it was obvious that he'd really hurt himself.

"Can you help him, Fairy Angora?" I whispered, but she shook her head sadly.

"Fairy magic doesn't work like that, dear one. He'll need proper treatment from a vet. And it's going to be quite a problem getting him away from his mother. We'd better hurry back and tell Lady Whitstable-Kent what's happened."

Chapter Four

We were all very quiet as the elephant slowly turned round. The lion cub was still struggling to get to his feet, and even the twins were looking anxious.

"There must be something we can do," I thought, and then I remembered Mia telling me about singing her little sister to sleep.

"Excuse me, Fairy Angora," I said, very quietly. "I know you said you couldn't mend the cub's leg...but what if we could take him to the vet ourselves? What if we could take him with us now?"

Fairy Angora looked surprised.

"But how could we do that, petal?"

I took a deep breath. "What if we persuaded the cubs and their mother to go to sleep? Could you do that with your magic? Then one of us could slip down and collect the little hurt one, and he'd have his leg seen to SO much sooner."

There was a long pause while Fairy Angora thought about what I'd said. At last she nodded.

"It would certainly be best to get him to the vet as soon as possible." She hesitated. "And I could make sure it was quite safe..."

"Oh, PLEASE, Fairy Angora!"

Gruella leant forward. "PLEASE can we try?"

I was amazed; I didn't think Gruella liked animals very much. And then I thought – perhaps she was feeling guilty. After all, if she hadn't shrieked with laughter the lion cub might not have fallen. Or was I just being mean? I decided to worry about the lion cub, not Gruella.

"I wondered if we could sing to them," I said, and Fairy Angora smiled at me.

"What a good idea! That would make my sleeping spell work perfectly. What should we sing?"

I looked at Mia. "What do you sing to your little sister?" I asked.

Mia grinned. "*Hush-a-bye Baby*. She loves that."

So we all began to sing, very very softly...

And Fairy Angora waved her wand very gently...

And soft white feathers floated up in the air and down onto the ground.

At first I thought nothing was

happening, but at last the lioness began to yawn, and the cub who was hurt stopped whimpering and curled up in a little ball. His sister patted at a feather or two, and then she curled up beside him.

Their mother yawned again, and stretched herself out on the ground. A moment later her eyelids closed, and she was asleep as well.

"Don't stop singing, princesses," Fairy Angora whispered. "You're doing wonderfully well." She leant forwards, and murmured in the elephant's ear, and our elephant began to move really, REALLY slowly towards the cubs. He stopped beside them, and I saw he was curling his trunk round towards me...and I knew what had to be done. I took a deep breath, and slid off the bench until I was balanced on his trunk...

and then he lowered me gently to the ground.

"Thank you," I whispered, and then bent and picked up the lion cub. He felt exactly like my cat at home, only much heavier, and I couldn't help kissing the top of his little furry head before I turned to climb back onto the elephant.

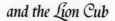

He curled his trunk into a step again, and Lindsey and Bethany reached down to take the little limp body safely out of my arms as I climbed up.

"Keep singing, dear ones," Fairy Angora instructed us as we settled the little cub on our laps, and we kept singing until we were right through the iron gates. Once we were on the other side and the gates were shut behind us Fairy Angora put her wand down, and I saw how pale she was.

"Are you all right?" I asked, and she smiled.

"I'm fine now," she said, "but I couldn't have done that spell without your help. You were all truly amazing. And now – let's get that little lion cub seen to!"

Chapter Five

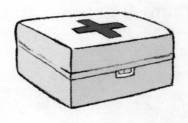

Lady Whit and King Percy were standing in the yard outside the veterinary centre when we came trundling up on our elephant, and they looked SO surprised to see us! King Percy began to frown, but once Fairy Angora had explained what had happened he clapped his hands in pleasure.

"Well done, princesses!" He beamed the hugest smile, and Lady Whit hurried the lion cub away into the centre to see the vet. "What excellent work!" King Percy continued. "I am delighted. I really am SO pleased, especially as I can see two princesses in your group that have been causing me some concern. Diamonde, Gruella – I think you know who I mean!"

I felt sure Diamonde would snigger and point at me, but she didn't. When I turned to look at her she was staring at the ground, and so was Gruella.

"I'm glad to see you looking ashamed of yourselves." King Percy folded his arms. "Yesterday afternoon Lady Whit and I were speaking of you. I remarked that I wished you were as thoughtful and kind as Princess Rebecca... and then I happened to glance in my study mirror. The two of you were listening at the open door!

Needless to say I was shocked to the core, but then Lady Whit persuaded me to give you one more chance. And it seems as if she was right." Our headteacher turned to Fairy Angora. "Am I right? Did the twins help to rescue the lion cub?"

Before Fairy Angora could say a word to King Percy, Diamonde stepped forward.

"Oh, we certainly did," she began, but Gruella gulped, and pushed her to one side.

She was blushing furiously as she stammered, "P-p-p-please, Your Majesty – it was Rebecca who saved him. Not us. It was her idea. And..." She blushed even more. "And...it was my fault he hurt himself and I'm really, REALLY sorry!" She burst into loud sobs, and hid her face in her hands. Diamonde hesitated, then put her arm round her sister.

Caitlin put up her hand. "Your Majesty – we don't know that for certain. His mother growled, and that could have made him lose his balance."

"That's true, Your Majesty," Lindsey said. "And it was Gruella who persuaded Fairy Angora to try the sleeping spell."

"Diamonde and Gruella both helped with the singing," Bethany added, while Mia and Abigail nodded.

King Percy threw back his head and laughed. "I see! All for one,

and one for all. Perfect princesses, all of you! Take twenty tiara points each, and I shall look forward enormously to presenting each one of you with your Diamond Sash at the end of term celebrations!"

Wasn't that just SO brilliant? We skipped and jumped round the yard, and Lindsey was whizzing round in her chair, until Fairy Angora asked us very nicely if we'd stop because the elephant was looking as if he was about to join in!

As we stopped, Lady Whit came round the corner carrying the little lion cub, who was still fast asleep – even though his paw had been neatly bandaged.

"I'm glad to say he'll be running and jumping again in just a day or two," she told us. "But if you hadn't brought him in so quickly

it could have been much worse.
Well done!" Then she actually
smiled, and handed me the cub.

"We thought you should take him back, Rebecca. You and Lindsey can go with Fairy Angora. You'll be quite safe, the lioness will still be asleep."

Lady Whit was right. As our elephant moved silently through the grass we saw the lioness lying where we'd left her, peacefully sleeping with her other cub beside her. As I slid off the elephant she stirred, but her eyes didn't open. I carefully put the cub beside his sister, and then the elephant lifted me up to the bench beside Lindsey...and the lioness woke up.

A moment later the cubs did too, and as we moved slowly away I saw the three of them nuzzling up together while the lioness purred and purred. And then she raised her huge head and looked straight at me, and I'm absolutely certain as certain can be that she knew exactly what had happened, and was grateful...

Chapter Six

Do you know something? That was the very best thing that happened to me at Diamond Turrets. Even when we all lined up at the end of term celebration and were presented with our Diamond Sashes I didn't feel hugely excited. When King Percy called me out and presented me with a special prize for being exceptionally thoughtful and brave I was very grateful, but I didn't particularly want to look at my prize. I just thought of that mother lion

looking at me, and thanking me
for taking care of her poor little
lion cub – well, little tingles went
up and down my spine.

*

It wasn't until after all the guests had gone home and we were in Tulip Room getting ready to go to bed that I remembered my prize.

"Probably a book," I thought as I tore off the paper, but it wasn't.

It was a picture; a picture of the lioness with her two cubs!

Lindsey smiled at me when I squeaked in excitement. "King Percy asked what we thought you'd like best," she said. "And we thought you'd like that..."

I threw my arms round her and hugged her, and then I hugged every single one of my friends, over and over again.

"It's the loveliest prize I could ever have," I told them, and then I hugged them again because they are just the BEST friends ever...

*

And I'm sending you a hug, too.
An enormous ELEPHANT-sized
hug...

And I'll see you very soon...
at Golden Gates!

Don't miss **Tiara** *The Club* *website at:*

www.tiaraclub.co.uk

Keep up to date with the latest
Tiara Club books and meet all
your favourite princesses!

There is SO much to see and do,
including games and activities. You can
even become an exclusive member of the
Tiara Club Princess Academy.

PLUS, there are exciting
competitions with truly
FABULOUS prizes!

Be a Perfect Princess – check it out today!

This s...

Rose Petal Picnic

Includes magical stickers!

The Tiara Club

Rose Petal Picnic

with Princess Anna & Princess Elizabeth

Vivian French

ISBN: 978 1 408 30579 9

Two stories in one fabulous book!

The Tiara Club books are priced at £3.99. *Butterfly Ball, Christmas Wonderland, Princess Parade, Emerald Ball, Midnight Masquerade* and *Rose Petal Picnic* are priced at £5.99. The Tiara Club books are available from all good bookshops, or can be ordered direct from the publisher: Orchard Books, PO BOX 29, Douglas IM99 1BQ.

Credit card orders please telephone 01624 836000 or fax 01624 837033 or visit our website: www.orchardbooks.co.uk or e-mail: bookshop@enterprise.net for details.

To order please quote title, author and ISBN and your full name and address.
Cheques and postal orders should be made payable to 'Bookpost plc.'
Postage and packing is FREE within the UK
(overseas customers should add £2.00 per book).
Prices and availability are subject to change.